Royalty

Kings and Queens

by Sally Lee

Consulting Editor: Gail Saunders-Smith, PhD

Consultant: Glenn A. Steinberg, PhD
Associate Professor of English
The College of New Jersey
Ewing, New Jersey

CAPSTONE PRESS
a capstone imprint

Pebble Plus is published by Capstone Press,
1710 Roe Crest Drive, North Mankato, Minnesota 56003
www.capstonepub.com

Library of Congress Cataloging-in-Publication Data
Lee, Sally.
  Kings and queens / by Sally Lee.
    p. cm.—(Pebble plus. Royalty)
  Includes bibliographical references and index.
  ISBN 978-1-62065-123-0 (library binding)
  ISBN 978-1-4765-1085-9 (eBook PDF)
1. Kings and rulers—Juvenile literature. 2. Queens—Juvenile literature. I. Title.
JC375.L435 2013
321'.6—dc23   2012030332

Editorial Credits
Erika L. Shores, editor; Juliette Peters, designer; Wanda Winch, media researcher; Jennifer Walker, production specialist

Photo Credits
Alamy Images: EPA/Sergio Barrenechea, 17; Corbis: Demotix/Azhar A Rahim, 5, dpa/Patrick van Katwijk, 1, Reuters/Toru Hanai, 19, Splash News, 15, VII Network/Lynsey Addario, 7; Getty Images, Inc: AFP, 11, AFP/Nasser Ayoub, 13, WPA/James Wiseman, 21; Newscom: picture-alliance/dpa/Carsten Rehder, 9; Rex USA: Rex/Will Schneider, cover; Shutterstock: Anna Subbotina, red satin design, Ecelop, gold swoosh design, hardtmuth, gold frame, mary416, cover castle

Note to Parents and Teachers

The Royalty set supports national social studies standards related to people, places, and culture. This book describes and illustrates kings and queens. The images support early readers in understanding the text. The repetition of words and phrases helps early readers learn new words. This book also introduces early readers to subject-specific vocabulary words, which are defined in the Glossary section. Early readers may need assistance to read some words and to use the Table of Contents, Glossary, Read More, Internet Sites, and Index sections of the book.

Printed in China.
092012   006934LEOS13

Table of Contents

What Are Kings and Queens?

Long ago, kings and queens were

the most powerful people

in all the land.

What is life like

for royal rulers today?

Malaysia's King Sultan Abdul Halim Mu'adzam Shah and Queen Sultanah Haminah Hamidun

Rulers such as kings and queens

are called monarchs.

They are not elected.

Most are the oldest child

of the previous monarch.

Bhutan's King Jigme Khesar Namgyel Wangchuck

What Do Kings and Queens Do?

Today most monarchs are symbols of their nations. People vote to elect government leaders who run the countries.

Sweden's Queen Silvia and King Carl XVI Gustaf

A few countries have
absolute monarchs.
Saudi Arabia's King Abdullah
has total control over the
government. His people don't vote.

Saudi Arabia's King Abdullah

Kings and queens meet often
with government leaders.
They go to events that raise money
for charities and important causes.

Jordan's Queen Rania
(white shirt) runs
in a charity race.

Monarchs promote their countries.

They visit other nations

and welcome important guests

at home.

England's Queen Elizabeth II and Prince Philip welcome U.S. President Barack Obama and First Lady Michelle Obama.

Meet the Kings and Queens

Juan Carlos I is the king of Spain.
His trips to represent Spain have
taken him to nearly every country.
The king is also the chief
of Spain's armed forces.

Emperor Akihito of Japan is
from the world's oldest
royal family.
He is also a scientist
who studies fish.

Japan's Emperor Akihito, Empress Michiko, and their family

Elizabeth II is queen of
the United Kingdom
and 15 other countries.
She lives in Buckingham Palace
in London.

Glossary

absolute monarch—a ruler who has all the power to run the government

armed forces—the whole military of a country

charity—a group that helps people in need

elect—to choose someone by voting

emperor—the male ruler of an empire or group of nations; equal to a king

government—the group of people who make laws, rules, and decisions for a country or state

monarch—a ruler such as a king, queen, or emperor

nation—to do with or belonging to a country as a whole

previous—coming just before another in time or order

promote—to advertise or show off good things about something

symbol—something that stands for something else

United Kingdom—a nation in Europe that includes England, Scotland, Wales, and Northern Ireland

Read More

Layne, Steven L., and Deborah Dover Layne. *P Is for Princess: A Royal Alphabet.* Chelsea, Mich.: Sleeping Bear Press, 2007.

Lee, Sally. *Castles and Palaces.* Royalty. North Mankato, Minn.: Capstone Press, 2013.

Roshell, Starshine. *Real-Life Royalty.* Reading Rocks! Mankato, Minn.: Child's World, 2008.

Internet Sites

FactHound offers a safe, fun way to find Internet sites related to this book. All of the sites on FactHound have been researched by our staff.

Here's all you do:

Visit *www.facthound.com*

Type in this code: 9781620651230

Super-cool stuff! Check out projects, games and lots more at **www.capstonekids.com**

Index

Word Count: 184
Grade: 1
Early-Intervention Level: 20